# Meeting Pickles

Story by Carmel Reilly

Illustrations by Pat Reynolds

## Contents

**Rigby**

HOUGHTON MIFFLIN HARCOURT
Supplemental Publishers

www.Rigby.com
800-531-5015

## Chapter 1

# The New Puppy

Eddie patted Pickles.

"Pickles is so funny," said Nina.
"He likes to play all the time."

Eddie was Nina's best friend.
He lived next door,
and he had come
to see Nina's new puppy.

Pickles jumped up
and barked at Eddie.

"Sit, Pickles," said Eddie. "Sit!"

But Pickles kept jumping up
and barking at him.

Nina laughed.
"He likes you, Eddie," she said.
"Come here, Pickles."

Pickles looked at Nina and barked.
Then he ran away.

Nina tried to catch him,
but every time she got close,
he would run away again.

Eddie began to chase Pickles, too.

## Chapter 2

# Too Fast

"Eddie, get Pickles!" cried Nina.
"Catch him before he goes inside the house!
Mom does not like him running
in the house."

They ran after Pickles,
but he was too fast for them.

Pickles raced up the steps
and in the back door.

"Oh, no!" Nina said to Eddie.
"We can't chase him inside the house.
Mom will be very mad at us!"

"She will be very mad at Pickles, too,"
said Eddie.

Suddenly,
Pickles came racing out of the house
with something in his mouth.

"Stop him, Eddie!" shouted Nina.
"What does he have in his mouth?"

"It's a shoe!" shouted Eddie.

"It's one of my **new** shoes,"
cried Nina.
"I left my shoes on the floor
by my backpack!"

## Chapter 3

# Put That Shoe Down!

Pickles sat down
and began to chew on Nina's shoe.

Nina walked slowly up to him.
"Pickles!" she said.
"Put my shoe down!
Good dog, Pickles."

Mom came out of the house
and saw Pickles with Nina's new shoe.
Mom was not happy at all.

"Pickles needs to go to puppy school,"
said Eddie.
Pickles looked at Eddie and barked.
Nina's shoe fell onto the grass.

"Yes," said Nina, laughing.
She picked up her shoe.
"We will have to take him to puppy school
as soon as we can!"